For Gijsbert – M.S.

Copyright © 2011 by Lemniscaat, Rotterdam, The Netherlands
First published in The Netherlands under the title *Beste Bregje Boentjes*
Text copyright © 2011 by Mathilde Stein
Illustration copyright © 2011 by Chuck Groenink
English translation copyright © 2012 by Lemniscaat USA LLC · New York
All rights reserved.

First published in the United States and Canada in 2012 by Lemniscaat USA LLC · New York
Distributed in the United States by Lemniscaat USA LLC · New York

Library of Congress Cataloging-in-Publication Data is available.
ISBN 13: 978-1-935954-18-7 (Hardcover)
Printing and binding: Worzalla, Stevens Point, WI USA
First U.S. edition

Mathilde Stein & Chuck Groenink

Lemniscaat

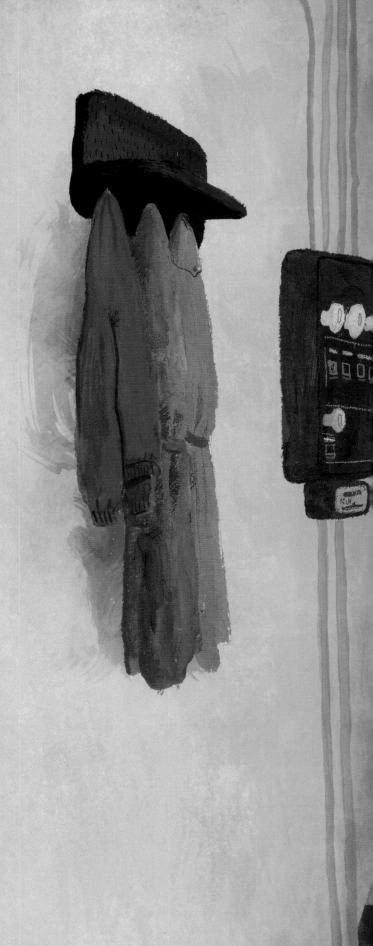

Wide-eyed Daisy stared at the envelope on the door-mat. A letter? For her? She read the name again. 'To Daisy D. Dunnington.' 'Daaaaaaaaisy!' an angry voice shouted from upstairs. 'Daisy, haven't you gone yet? When will you learn to hurry! Remember there's more work waiting for you when you get back. Now move it! And don't you dare to go out without your coat. And don't forget to take the shopping bag, and make sure I don't see you talking to strangers, and...' Daisy was only half listening. With trembling hands, she picked up the letter. Who could it be from? Suppose... just suppose...

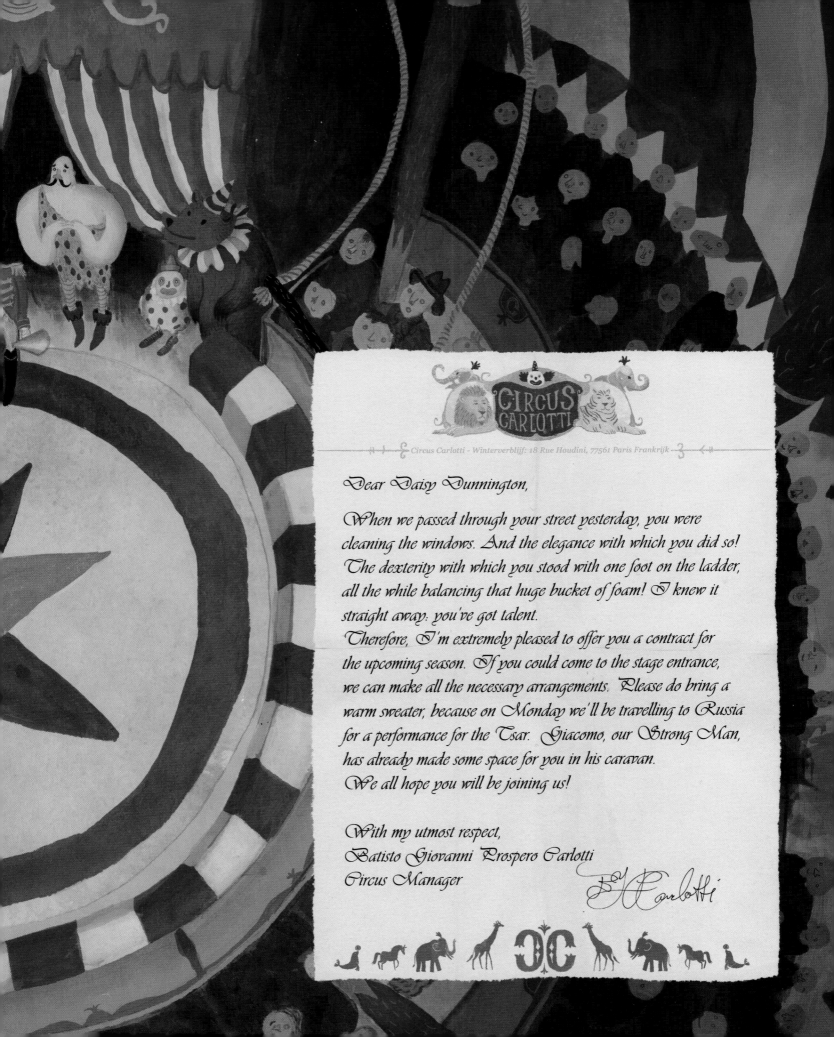

CIRCUS CARLOTTI

Circus Carlotti - Winterverblijf: 18 Rue Houdini, 77561 Paris Frankrijk

Dear Daisy Dunnington,

When we passed through your street yesterday, you were
cleaning the windows. And the elegance with which you did so!
The dexterity with which you stood with one foot on the ladder,
all the while balancing that huge bucket of foam! I knew it
straight away: you've got talent.
Therefore, I'm extremely pleased to offer you a contract for
the upcoming season. If you could come to the stage entrance,
we can make all the necessary arrangements. Please do bring a
warm sweater, because on Monday we'll be travelling to Russia
for a performance for the Tsar. Giacomo, our Strong Man,
has already made some space for you in his caravan.
We all hope you will be joining us!

With my utmost respect,
Batisto Giovanni Prospero Carlotti
Circus Manager

Dear, dear Miss Dunnington,

Oh, those lovely bright eyes! That wonderful shine in your
hair! The music of your voice! Ever since my cousin Abdul,
your vegetable man on the market, has told me about you, my
heart has yearned for you. At night I can only dream about
you. Dear Miss Dunnington, I beg you: give me your hand in
marriage and let us light the stars in the sky together...
This Saturday, I will send my magic carpet to collect you.
Please do not worry about what clothes to bring because I
will buy you a brand new wardrobe — with an extra toothbrush
as well. Oh, dear Miss Dunnington, I can hardly wait until I
hold you in my arms...

Your devoted
Sheik Abu Dhabi

Hi Daisy!

Remember me? This is Alice, the girl who used to live next door to you - until I moved to Peru that is. I have been in the jungle for months now trying to discover the mysterious Wiggly Wonky monkey with my expedition team. It is absolutely fantabulous!

Now listen to this: One of my colleagues has just been sent home. He turned out to be allergic to jungle seeds, and sneezed so loud that he kept scaring the animals away. So I was thinking... are you still quiet as a church mouse? And could you get away from home for a while? If so, do please hop onto the next plane - I'm sure you'll be a terrific help!

Much love,
Alice xxx

O.R.H. Daiselia Delphinia
Desdemona Dunnington

We are tremendously sorry, but we have just discovered a very regrettable mistake. At the time of your birth, you were accidentally 'swapped' in the hospital. Your mother is not your mother! Indeed, your true mother is the Queen.

We understand this news must be a terrible shock for you, and do apologize profusely. However, the Queen would like to welcome you back into the family as soon as possible. Would it be convenient if she personally came to collect you with the royal coach tomorrow? This way, you could begin with tea together in the Palace, and perhaps you would see fit to discuss the decoration for your new room on the same occasion.

I'm looking forward to waiting on you,

Alexander Grimples

Sir Hubert Tatter Tawdry-Tout
Your future servant

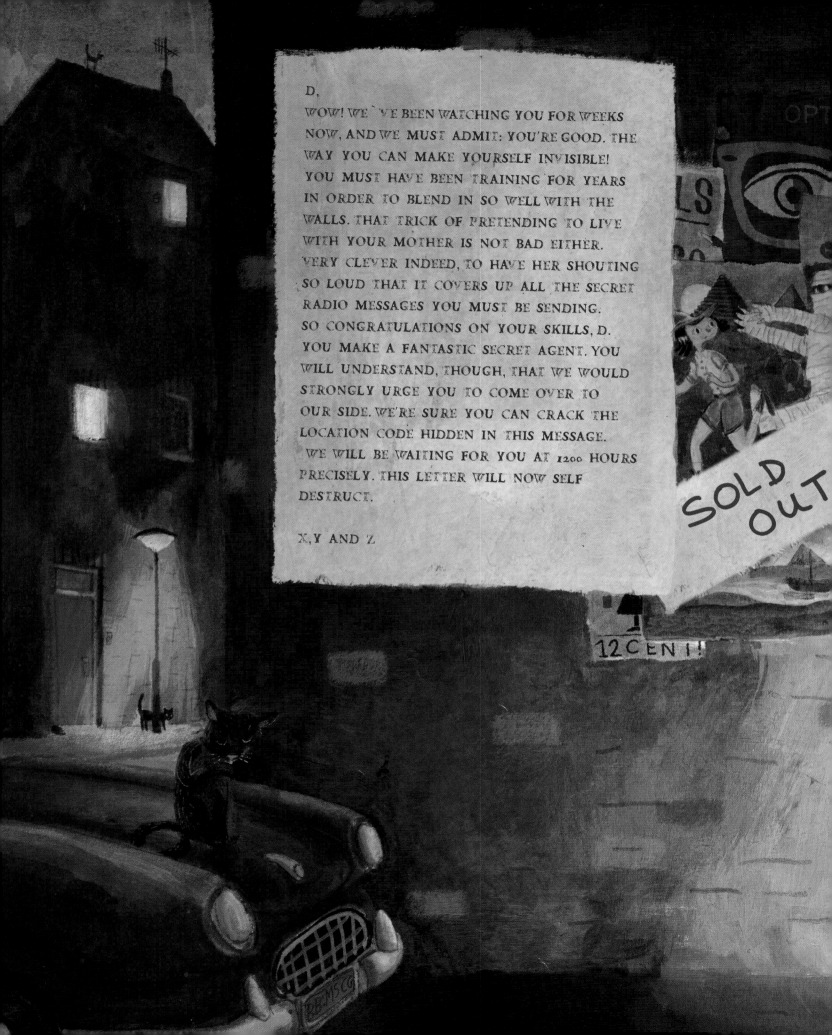

D,

WOW! WE'VE BEEN WATCHING YOU FOR WEEKS NOW, AND WE MUST ADMIT: YOU'RE GOOD. THE WAY YOU CAN MAKE YOURSELF INVISIBLE! YOU MUST HAVE BEEN TRAINING FOR YEARS IN ORDER TO BLEND IN SO WELL WITH THE WALLS. THAT TRICK OF PRETENDING TO LIVE WITH YOUR MOTHER IS NOT BAD EITHER. VERY CLEVER INDEED, TO HAVE HER SHOUTING SO LOUD THAT IT COVERS UP ALL THE SECRET RADIO MESSAGES YOU MUST BE SENDING. SO CONGRATULATIONS ON YOUR SKILLS, D. YOU MAKE A FANTASTIC SECRET AGENT. YOU WILL UNDERSTAND, THOUGH, THAT WE WOULD STRONGLY URGE YOU TO COME OVER TO OUR SIDE. WE'RE SURE YOU CAN CRACK THE LOCATION CODE HIDDEN IN THIS MESSAGE. WE WILL BE WAITING FOR YOU AT 1200 HOURS PRECISELY. THIS LETTER WILL NOW SELF DESTRUCT.

X, Y AND Z

Dear Daisy Dunnington,

It's with great regret that we have to inform you that your great-great-grand uncle, Sir Preston 'Bubble' Jones, passed away last month during his attempt to break the world record in bubble blowing.
Your great-great-grand uncle's will show you to be his only heir.
As far as we can foresee at present, his fortune amounts to three gazillion-seven billion and four hundred-eighty-eight million dollar.
This is of course still without taking into account his possessions in New York, Texas and Kippletown, as well as the estimated benefits from the Preston Candy Plant.
Would you be kind enough to inform us of your personal banking number, so that we can transfer the afore-mentioned funds as soon as possible?

Our thoughts are with you at this sad time.

With our deepest compassion,
Mr. Peter Pringle

Pringle & Luckhurst associates
United States

Dear Daisy Dunnington,

Oh, what a discovery! I hope you will forgive me for having followed you secretly yesterday, but I simply had to know where you lived. I've been searching for months. I've auditioned hundreds of actresses, each outshining the other with the whiteness of their teeth, the luster of their hair, the interminable length of their legs... But, Daisy dear, sometimes beauty is not enough. In my films I want character! Passion! Despair! And just when I was about to abandon my quest... Daisy Dunnington, there you were! In the supermarket – as simple as that! I can still hardly believe my luck. It's you – you have it. Please accept the leading part in my latest film. With a star like you, we can surely make 'The Wrath of the Mummy' a worldwide hit.

I look forward to working with you, Daisy darling!

Mel Glitzstein

Mel Glitzstein

Darling Daisy,

Whenever I see you walk past in the street
My heart skips a beat 'cause you're ever so sweet
I'm longing to greet you each time you go by
If only I weren't so terribly shy...
But just when I think that for once I will dare
There's always your mom, with that horrible glare
Oh Daisy, I loathe her! That woman is vile!
Always shouting at you, and never a smile...
I would love to banish your worries and cares
And get you away from that dragon upstairs.
So, I beg you Daisy, please may it be me:
The person whose mother-in-law she shall be....

Anonymous

'Daisy! Daisy, you good-for-nothing, are you still standing there? You know that I want my dinner at 6:30 precisely!'

With a start, Daisy lifted her head. 'Yes, m-m-mother,' she stammered. 'I'm going.' She glanced at the dark staircase one more time. Then she took a deep breath, straightened her back, and gripped the envelope firmly in her hand. 'Yes ma'am,' she said again. 'I am going.'

And off she went.

Without her coat, without her bag – but with a twinkle in her eye.